FUN HOME

A NEW BROADWAY MUSICAL

MUSIC BY
JEANINE TESORI

BOOK AND LYRICS BY
LISA KRON

BASED ON THE GRAPHIC NOVEL BY
ALISON BECHDEL

SAMUEL FRENCH

CONTENTS

THE BROADWAY CAST OF "FUN HOME"
PHOTO BY JOAN MARCUS

BETH MALONE
PHOTO BY JOAN MARCUS

FOREWORD

I offer here a few thoughts on the dramatic construction of our musical, *Fun Home*, in the hope that they might be useful to you in interpreting this material.

Our central goal in adapting Alison Bechdel's graphic novel into a musical was to transform a story about things that happened in the past into a drama peopled by characters moving forward in time. As Thornton Wilder says, "A novel is what took place [but] on the stage it is always now: the personages are standing on that razor-edge between the past and the future...the words are rising to their lips in immediate spontaneity."

But, you may wonder, isn't adult Alison looking back? Doesn't she tell us at the top of the show what's going to happen to her dad?

Well, yes and no. At the end of the song "Welcome to Our House," she does say, "My father and I both grew up in the same Pennsylvania town. And he was gay. And I was gay. And he killed himself. And I became a lesbian cartoonist." Alison isn't telling these things to the audience. She doesn't know about the audience. She's not a narrator. She's a character, doggedly pursuing a goal as characters do, combing through her past on a hunt to piece together a truer version of her father's life than the one she's hung on to since he died. She's an artist, so she figures things out by sketching, drafting, trying out ideas, trying out captions, rejecting them, refining them, and reshaping them as new information comes in. Though she often speaks in declarative sentences, she's never giving exposition; she's always trying to figure something out by laying out facts that don't add up in a search for some key point she's missed. Why, when she and her father were so much alike, did they have such different fates? When did their paths diverge? Why did he kill himself?

Her work, at the top of the piece, is an intellectual and artistic quest: She tells us that she "can't abide romantic notions" of the past and is determined to "know what's true/dig deep into who and what and why and when." Her imperative to follow the path of truth wherever it leads, though, soon draws her away from her intellectual safety zone into an utterly unfamiliar whirl of unprocessed emotion. Though she tries again and again to use her tried and true work methods to keep control of the situation, it's not enough, and finally she tumbles over the edge into a fully felt reckoning with the moment of her father's death.

How do the other characters fit into her search?

Alison's search calls forth the other two time periods: Alison as a child, and Alison as a college student. But these scenes flow unbidden and on their own terms, as memories do. Another way of saying this is that the past always understands itself to be the present. And while Alison can speak to the past, the past is oblivious to her.

Every character in this piece is moving earnestly forward at all times into an unknown and unknowable future. This is very important. It's tempting to let an elegiac tone or a sense of foreboding start to creep into the piece. It's tempting for actors to want to play impending sadness. It can be hard to trust that the story will be sad if the characters in it don't know it's going to be sad. But it's the characters' innocence of what lies ahead that allows the audience to feel the pressure and poignancy of what's coming. We had a lightning-bolt moment in this regard during the writing process when we realized that we had initially written Medium Alison's coming-out scene with a melancholy tone. That would be how adult Alison would remember those events: as the catalyst for her father's suicide. But we realized that the nineteen-year-old moving forward in time wouldn't have those associations. We re-wrote the scene, far more effectively, as a joyful opening into a world of wondrous possibility.

It is also important to resist any impulse to draw a narrative arc through the family scenes, or imply in any way a causal chain of events leading to Bruce's suicide. Each scene from the past should be played for whatever daily stakes exist in the scene itself. This might feel counterintuitive, but the narrative arc of this musical is located not in the scenes from the past, but with adult Alison. It's her present-tense assembly and interrogation of these memories that we're following. That location of the narrative spine with adult Alison, along with the past's innocence of the future, is what makes this musical cohere and come alive.

Lisa Kron, April 2016

It All Comes Back

(Opening)

Music: Jeanine Tesori
Lyrics: Lisa Kron

SMALL ALISON *parlando*

B(sus2)/D♯

Dad - dy, hey Dad - dy, come here, o - kay? I need you.

colla voce

B(sus2)/E

What are you do - ing? I said come here! You need to do what I tell you to do

Lis-ten to me. Dad-dy! Come here, hey, right here, right now, you're mak-ing me mad.

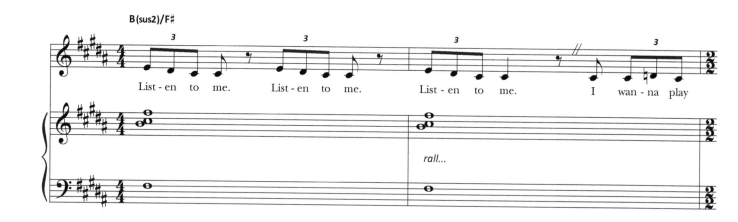

B(sus2)/F♯

List - en to me. List - en to me. List - en to me. I wan - na play

rall...

♩ = 76

A   D♭

air - plane   I wan-na play   air - plane   I wan-na play

cresc.

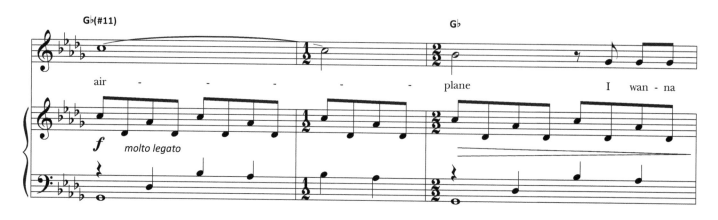

G♭(♯11)   G♭

air - - - - - plane   I wan - na

𝆑 molto legato

4

BRUCE. It's from Clyde Gibbon's barn. What a haul. He said, "Take what you want," and I said, "You sure, Clyde?"

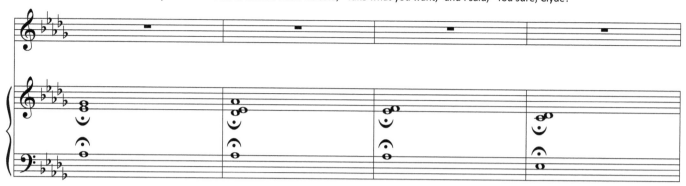

BRUCE. He said, "It's all junk to me," so I said, "Alright, Clyde. Alright." Come here. Look. (**SMALL ALISON** *looks on as he combs through the box.*)

BRUCE. You go to auctions, yard sales, comb the dump and crap, there's crap, there's crap there's—

(He pulls out a wrinkled wad of cloth.)
BRUCE. Ah! What's this?
SMALL ALISON. More crap?

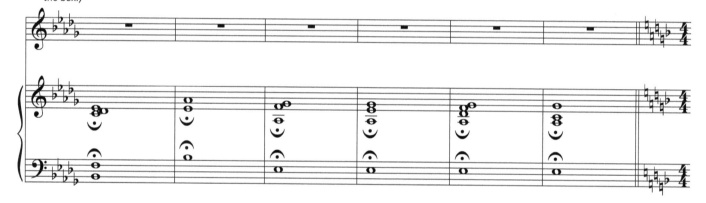

♩ = 88

BRUCE. *(Rapturously inspecting the wadded fabric.)* No—

5

lus - ter   And the mark, is there a mark?   Yes, this

stamp, you see__ right here?   That's how the crafts - man__ leaves a sign   that

he was here__ and made his work__   so

8

back There's you and there's me But now I'm the one— who's

for-ty - three and stuck I can't find my way— through _____

ALISON

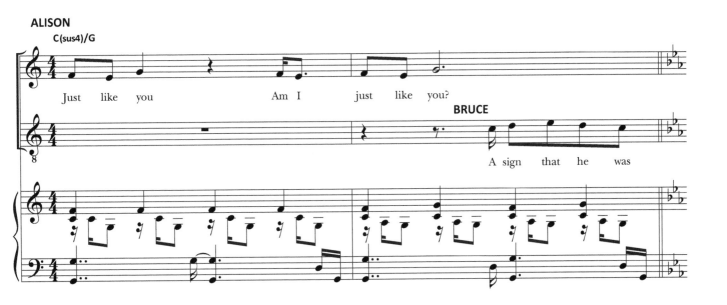

Just like you Am I just like you?

BRUCE

A sign that he was

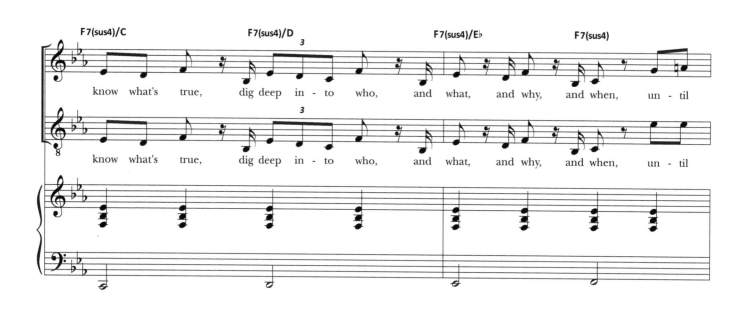

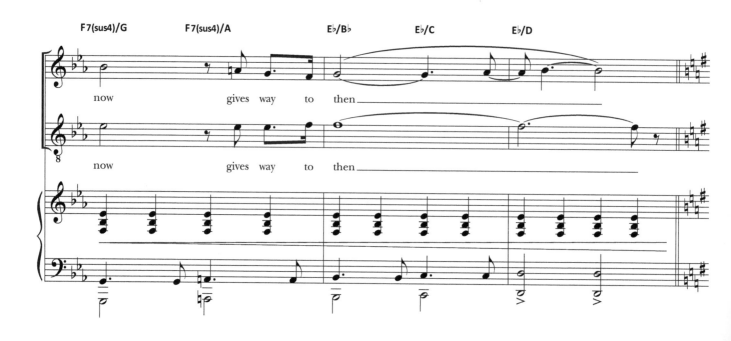

14

Welcome to Our House on Maple Avenue

Music: Jeanine Tesori
Lyrics: Lisa Kron

18

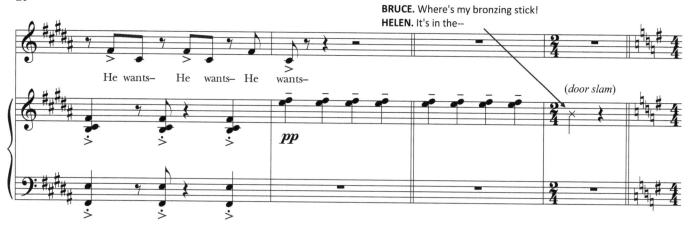

BRUCE. Where's my bronzing stick!
HELEN. It's in the--

He wants— He wants— He wants—

(door slam)

Calmly, observing with interest

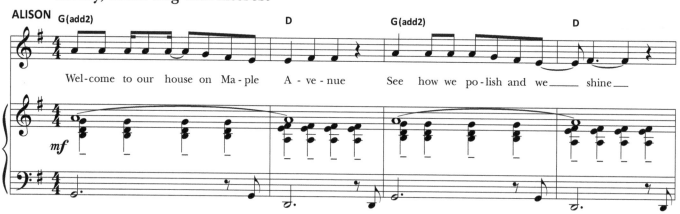

Wel-come to our house on Ma-ple A-ve-nue See how we po-lish and we_____ shine_____

We re-ar-range and re-a - lign_____ Ev-'ry-thing is bal-anced and se-rene like
more

ALISON and HELEN

cha-os ne-ver hap-pens if it's ne - ver seen_____ Ev-'ry need we an-ti-ci-pate and

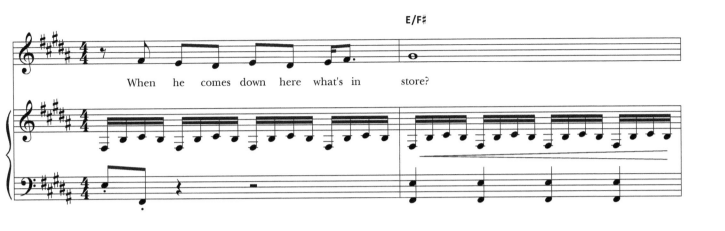

When he comes down here what's in store?

HELEN and KIDS

He wants— He wants— He wants—

HELEN, CHRISTIAN, and JOHN

Wel - come to our house on Ma - ple A - ve - nue

ALISON and SMALL ALISON

Wel - come to our house on Ma - ple

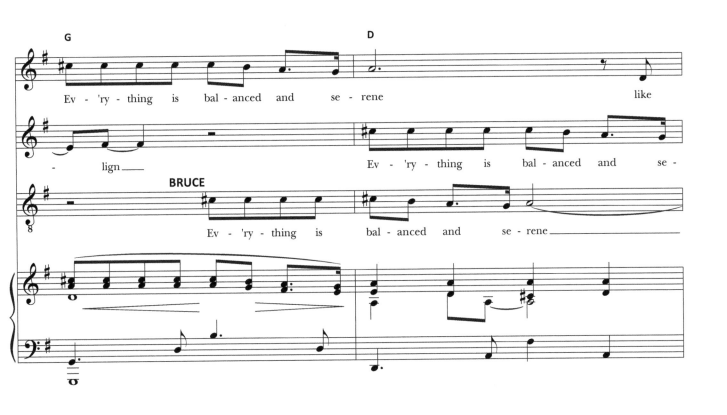

G/A

HELEN

ALL EXCEPT ALISON

And ___ yet— ___

ty - pi - cal ___ fam - i - ly ___ quin - tet ___

Slower (♩=76)

BRUCE

Not too ___ bad, if I say so ___ my - self I might still ___ break a heart or ___ two ___

mp gently

molto esp.

♩=104

B m(add9)

ten.

Some - times the fi - re burns so hot I don't know what I'll do

sub. f

Not too ___ bad, ___ if I say so ___ my - self

Tempo Primo

ALISON

Not too bad ___

BRUCE

Not too bad ___

BRUCE. Mrs. Bochner, pleasure to meet you, come on in!

HELEN and KIDS

BRUCE. Thank you. Obviously still a work in progress. Oh yes, I've done all the work myself.

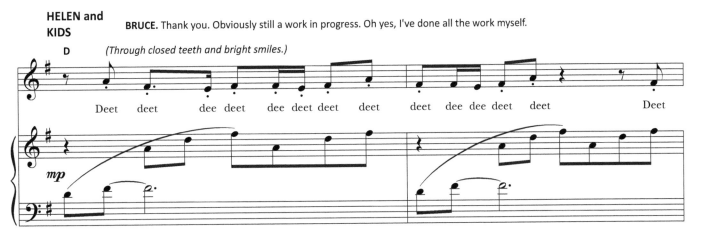

(Through closed teeth and bright smiles.)

Deet deet dee deet dee deet deet deet deet dee dee deet deet Deet

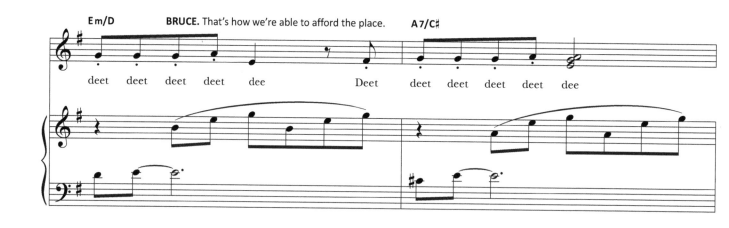

Em/D   **BRUCE.** That's how we're able to afford the place.   A7/C#

deet   deet   deet   deet   dee   Deet   deet   deet   deet   deet   dee

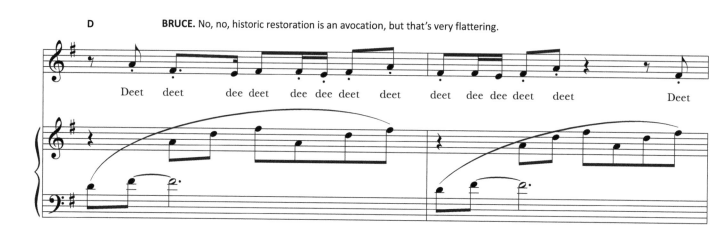

D   **BRUCE.** No, no, historic restoration is an avocation, but that's very flattering.

Deet   deet   dee deet   dee dee deet   deet   deet   dee dee deet   deet   Deet

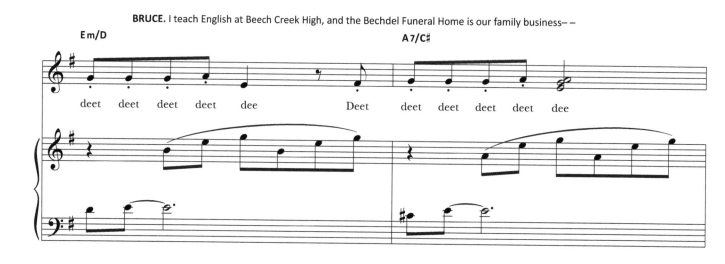

BRUCE. I teach English at Beech Creek High, and the Bechdel Funeral Home is our family business– –

Em/D   A7/C#

deet   deet   deet   deet   dee   Deet   deet   deet   deet   deet   dee

(ROY steps into the house, young, handsome, and dressed for yard work.)
ROY. Anybody home?

*(The camera FLASHES, capturing **BRUCE**, posed with his family, gazing at the young man.)*

ALISON

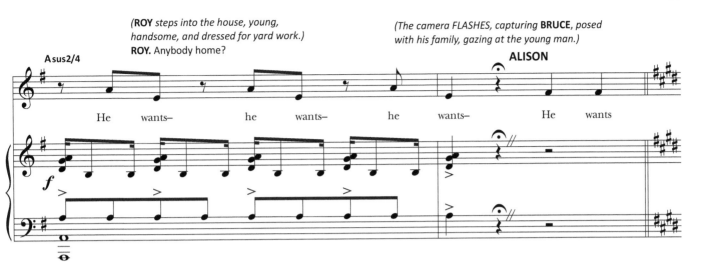

He wants— he wants— he wants— He wants

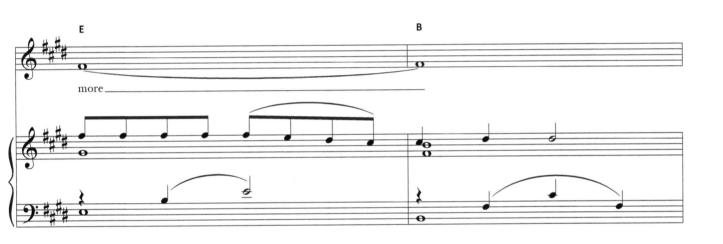

more _____

ALISON. Caption: My dad and
I grew up in the same small
Pennsylvania town
And he was gay
And I was gay
And he killed himself

ALISON. And I became a
lesbian cartoonist.

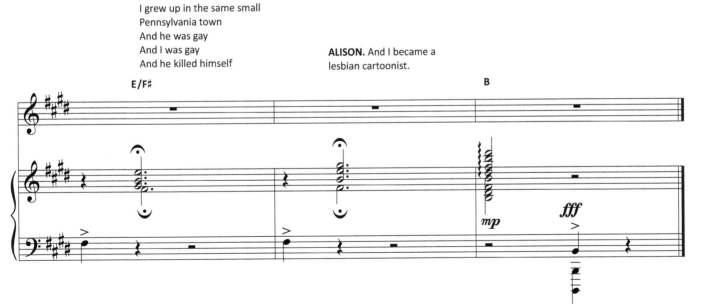

Come to the Fun Home

Music: Jeanine Tesori
Lyrics: Lisa Kron

Funky Jackson 5
In 2 (♩ = 94)

JOHN
Your un-cle died___ You're feel-in' low - oo

You've got_ to bu - ry your ma - ma but you don't know where_ to go_

Your pa - pa needs his fi - nal rest_

You got you got you got to give them the best Oh_____

34

You've got no rea-son to roam _____ Use the Bech-del Fu-ner-al

Home What it is What it is Hoo hoo hoo What it is What it is now, ba-beh

JOHN

Oh oo oh oo Here come da judge Here come _____ da judge, ba-beh

SMALL ALISON

Sock it to me   Sock it to me   Sock it to me   Sock it to me ba-beh

CHRISTIAN

Sock it to me   Sock it to me   Sock it to me   Sock it to me ba-beh

Changing My Major

Music: Jeanine Tesori
Lyrics: Lisa Kron

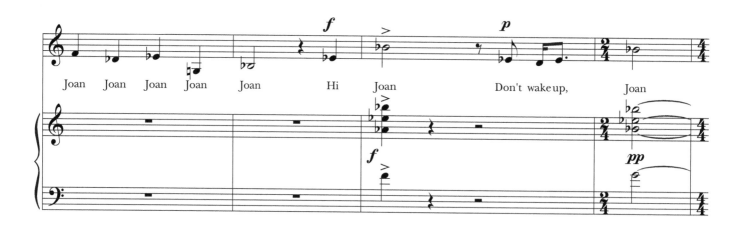

Neurotic, a little too fast, <u>Not Rubato</u>

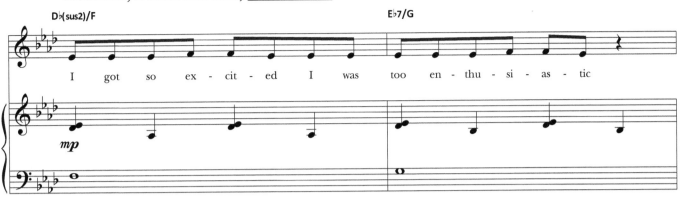

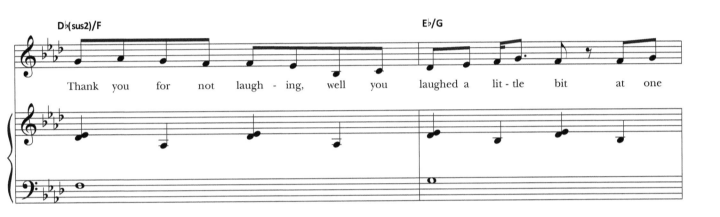

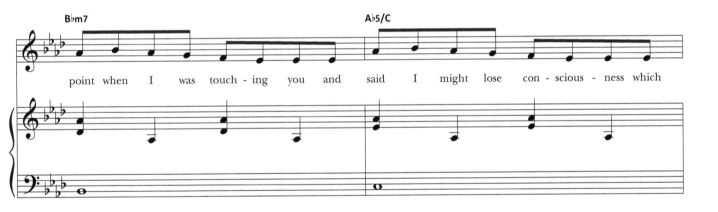

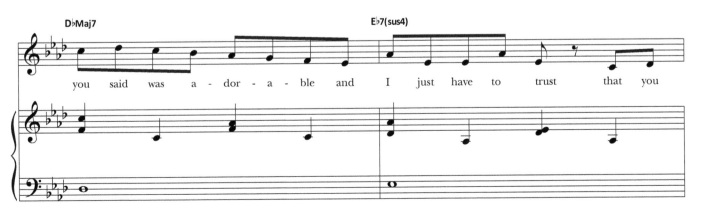

44

don't think I'm an i - di - ot___ or some kind of an an - i - mal I

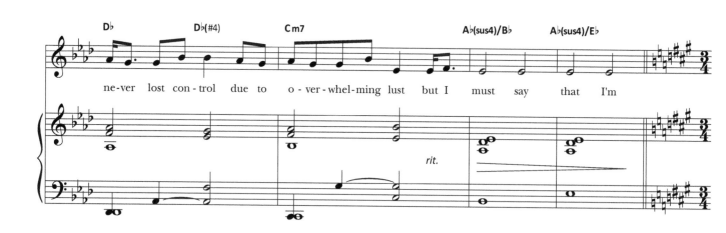

ne - ver lost con - trol due to o - ver - whel - ming lust but I must say that I'm

Waltz, in 1 (.=48-50)

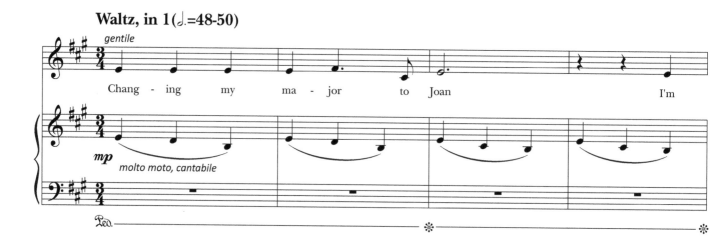

Chang - ing my ma - jor to Joan I'm

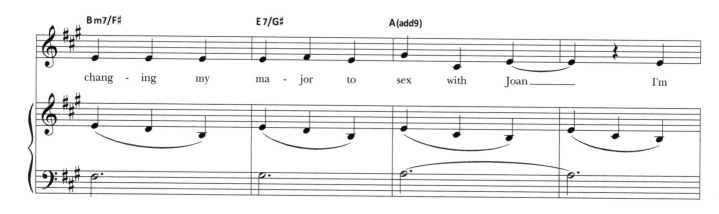

chang - ing my ma - jor to sex with Joan___ I'm

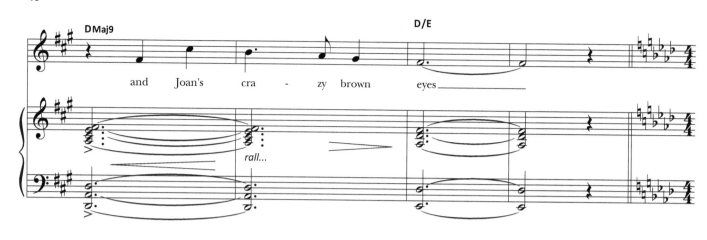

and Joan's cra - zy brown eyes _____

Tempo primo, sempre non rubato

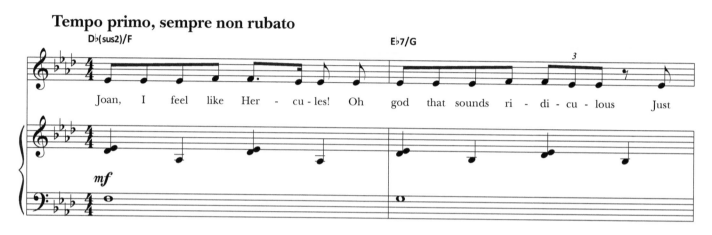

Joan, I feel like Her - cu - les! Oh god that sounds ri - di - cu - lous Just

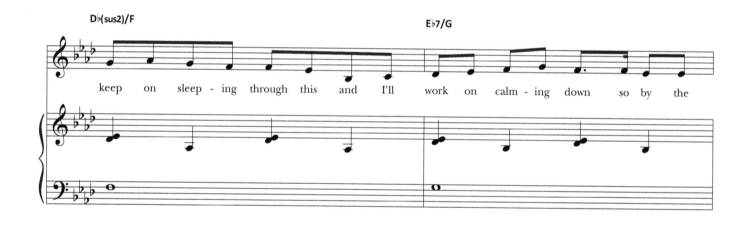

keep on sleep - ing through this and I'll work on calm - ing down so by the

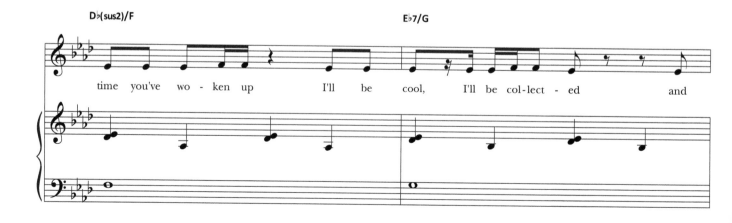

time you've wo - ken up I'll be cool, I'll be col - lect - ed and

Giddy, silly

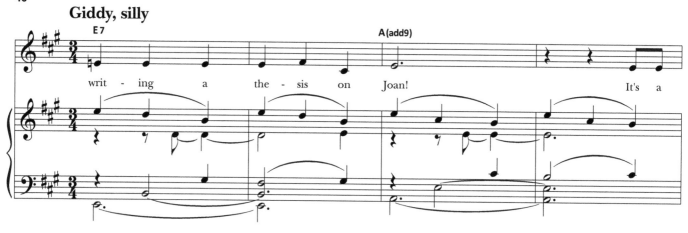

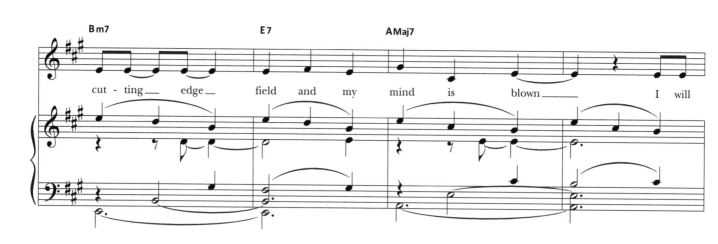

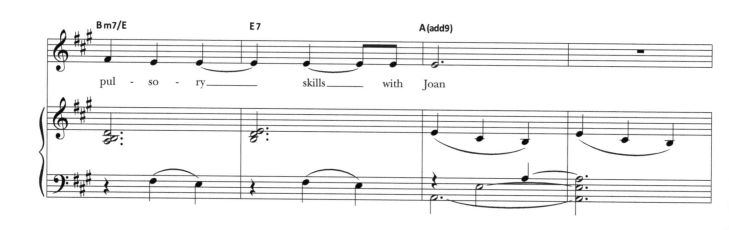

50

Faster

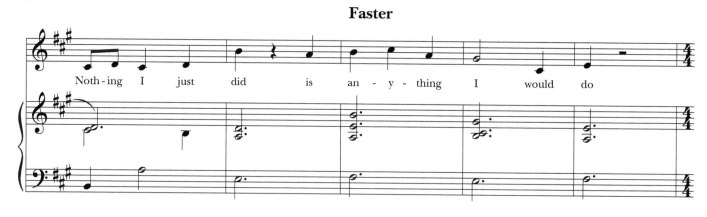

Noth-ing I just did is an-y-thing I would do

O-ver-night ev-'ry-thing changed I am not pre-pared. I'm diz-zy I'm naus-eous I'm shak-y I'm

C#m9

(Genuinely asking.)

scared _____ Am I _____

accel.

In 2

F 7(#11)

G/D

fall-ing in-to noth-ing-ness or fly-ing in-to some-thing so sub-

Definite, sure ("to the world!") - In 4

52

Maps

Music: Jeanine Tesori
Lyrics: Lisa Kron

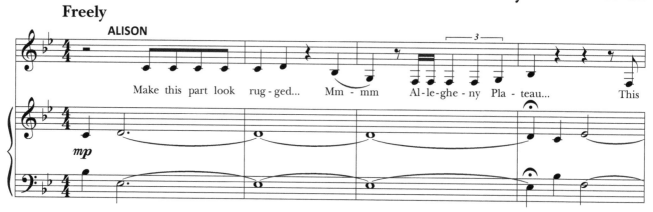

Not gently, with purpose

Quick dash - es mark___ the pro - per-ty ends Beech Creek, a rope that turns and bends

Lit - tle squares for hous - es strung a - long roads___

The land trans - fig - ured in - to top - o - graph - ic codes

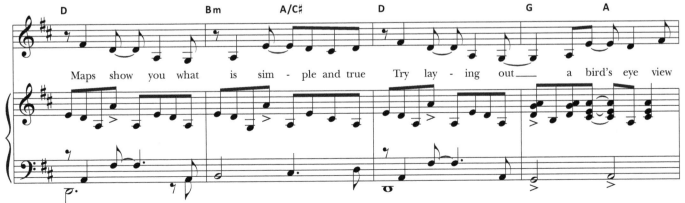

Maps show you what is sim - ple and true Try lay - ing out___ a bird's eye view

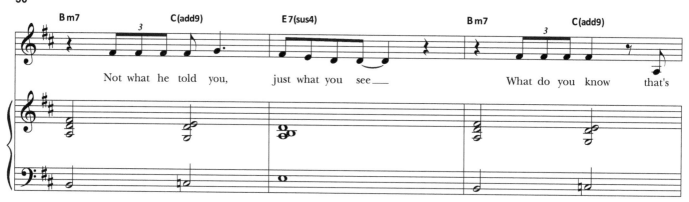

Not what he told you, just what you see___ What do you know that's

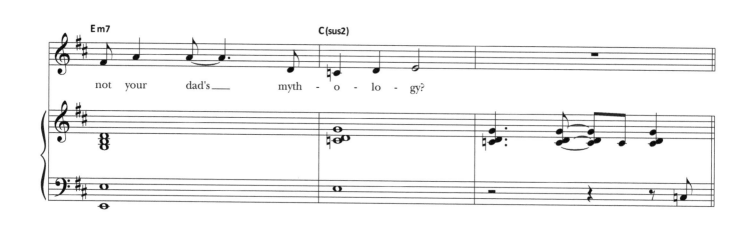

not your dad's___ myth - o - lo - gy?

Dad was born on this farm___ Here's our house Here's the spot___ where he died

I can draw a cir - cle His whole life fits in - side

58

Raincoat of Love

Music: Jeanine Tesori
Lyrics: Lisa Kron

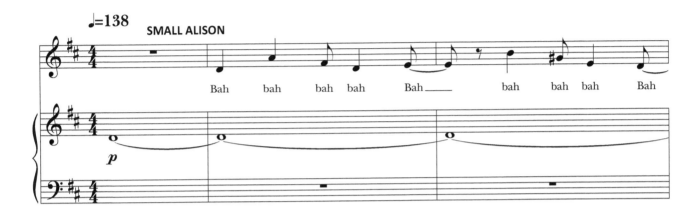

BOBBY JEREMY

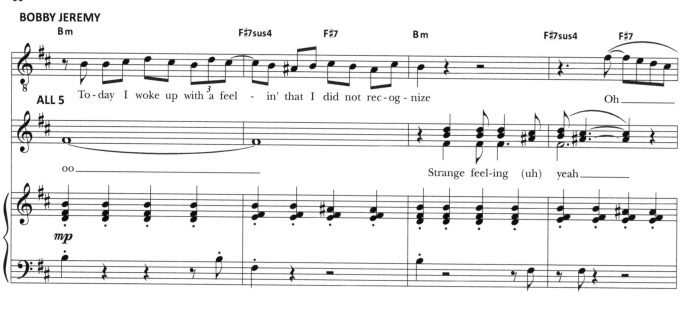

ALL 5

To-day I woke up with a feel - in' that I did not rec-og-nize

oo

Oh ___

Strange feel-ing (uh) yeah ___

___ Our hap-py life seemed far a-way and ev-'ry-thing was made of ___ lies ___

oo ___

The

Lies yeah ___

sky was turn-ing dark when, ba - by, I looked ___ in your eyes ___

oo oo ___ oo oo

ah ___

(ossia)

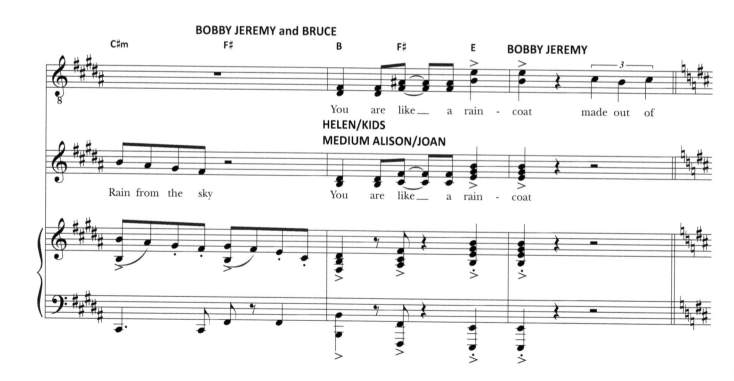

Ring of Keys

Music: Jeanine Tesori
Lyrics: Lisa Kron

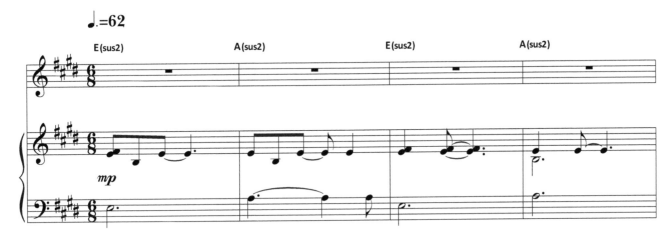

SMALL ALISON

Some-one just came in the door   Like no one I ev - er saw be-fore___ I feel–

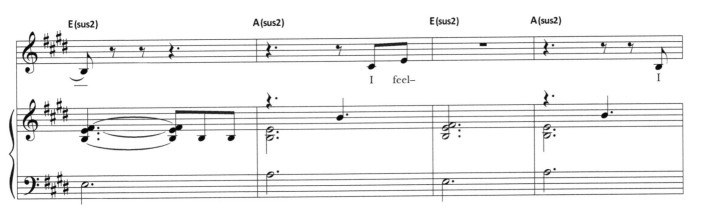

I feel–   I

don't know where you came from I wish I did, I feel so dumb, I feel– Your

swag-ger___ and your bear-ing___ and the just - right clothes you're wear-ing___ Your

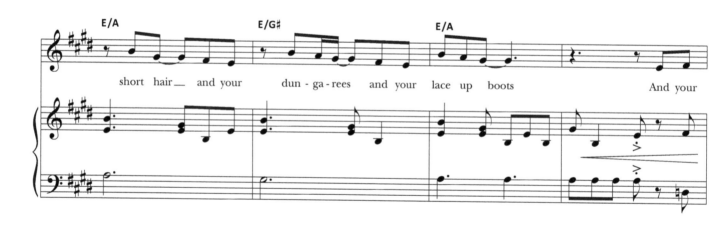

short hair___ and your dun - ga-rees and your lace up boots And your

keys, oh,_____ your ring of keys

Groove

72

Days and Days

Music: Jeanine Tesori
Lyrics: Lisa Kron

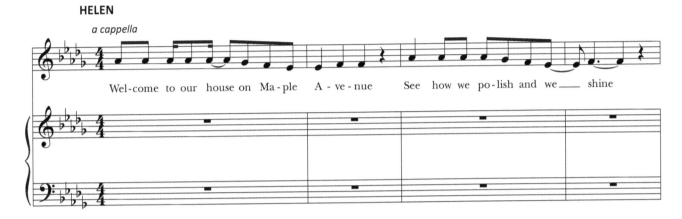

Wel-come to our house on Ma-ple A-ve-nue   See how we po-lish and we____ shine

We re-ar-range and re-a-lign____   Ev-'ry-thing is bal-anced and– and–

Tempo Moderato

Days and days and days, that's how it hap-pens Days and days and days   Made of

76

molto cresc. poco a poco

Days and days and days and days and days and days and days

mf

relentless

molto rall...

Regal, biting

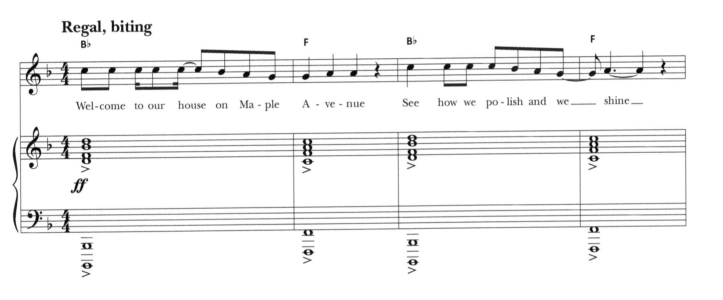

Bb   F   Bb   F

Wel-come to our house on Ma - ple A - ve - nue   See how we po-lish and we ___ shine ___

ff

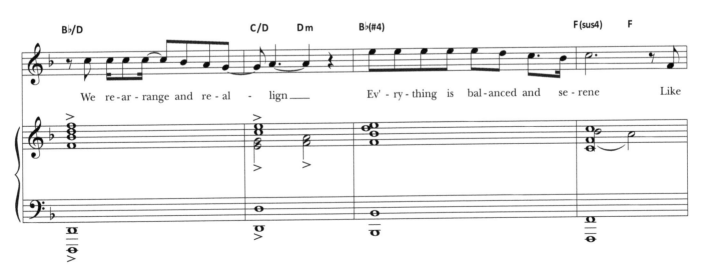

Bb/D   C/D   Dm   Bb(#4)   F(sus4)   F

We re-ar - range and re-al - lign ___   Ev' - ry - thing is bal-anced and se - rene   Like

Telephone Wire

Music: Jeanine Tesori
Lyrics: Lisa Kron

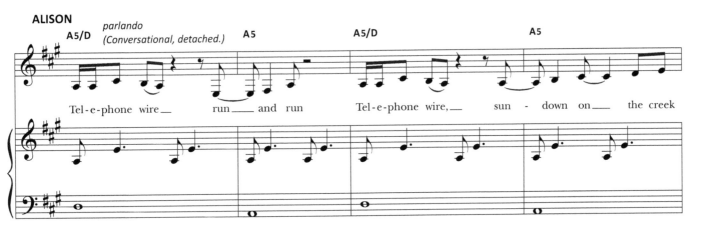

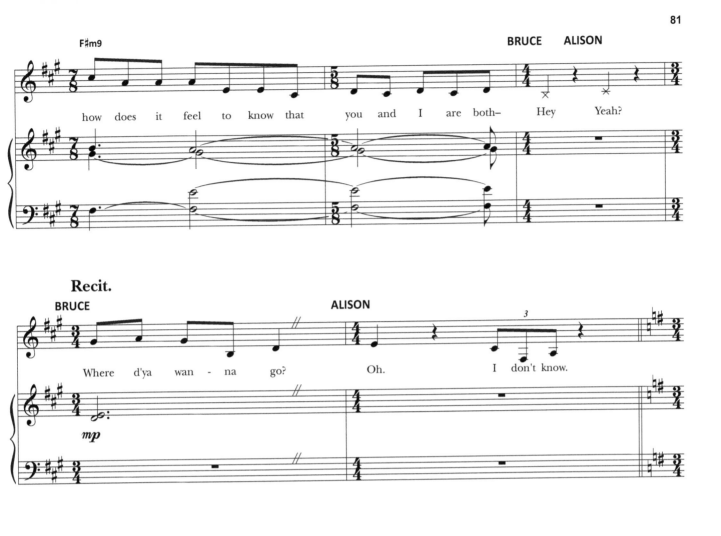

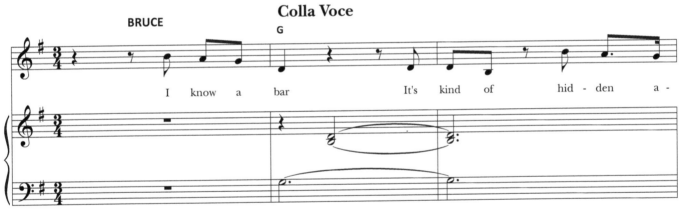

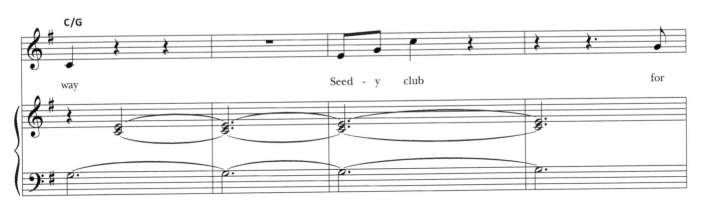

folks like, you know   Could be fun   But

Faster recit.

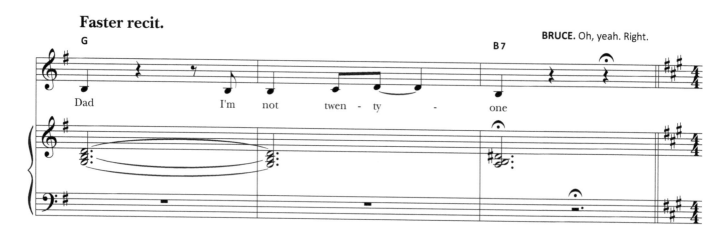

BRUCE. Oh, yeah. Right.

Dad   I'm not   twen - ty - one

Tempo Primo (♩=120)

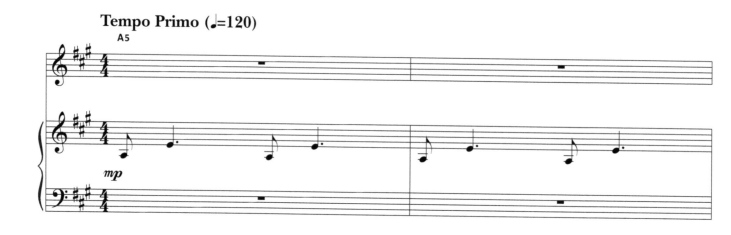

ALISON   *parlando*
(Conversational, detached.)

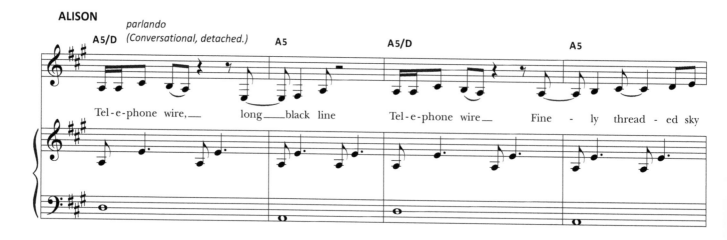

Tel - e - phone wire,___   long___black line   Tel - e - phone wire___   Fine - ly thread - ed sky

At the light at the light at the light at the light___ Does-n't mat-

Recit, quick

ter what you say___ Just make the fear in his eyes go a-way_____ There was a

Colla Voce

boy In col-lege My first year there

Nor-ris Jones He had black wa-vy hair_____

BRUCE. Huh.

86

Subito Allegro (♩=150)

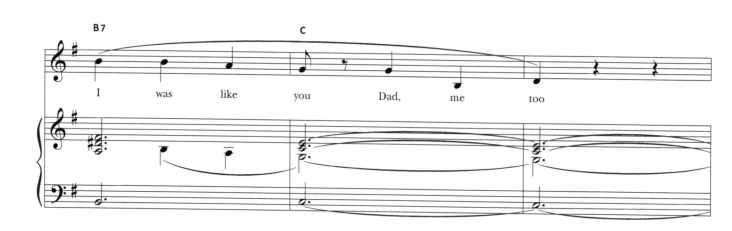

Freely

BRUCE

ALISON. Dad?

ALISON. Dad?

Nor - ris Jones

Nor - ris Jones

BRUCE. Did I mention I've taken on a new project?
That old house out on Route 150! You've seen it,
Al. It's been sitting empty out there for forty,
fifty years at least.

Tempo Primo

ALISON

Tel - e-phone wire___ Stop!___ Too fast!___

Tel - e-phone wire___ Make___ this not___ the past, this car ride!

This is where it has to hap - pen There must be some o-ther chan - ces There's a mo-ment I'm for-

88

Edges of the World

Music: Jeanine Tesori
Lyrics: Lisa Kron

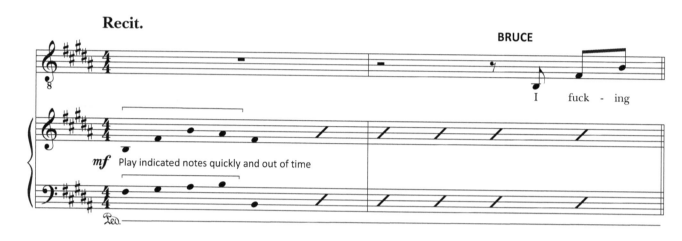

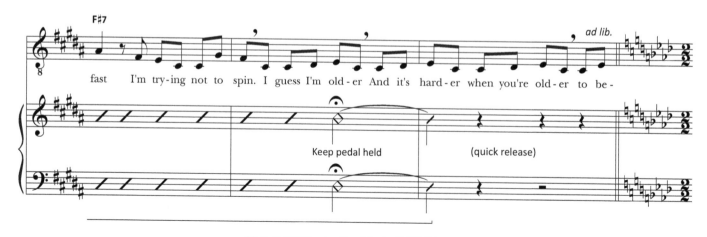

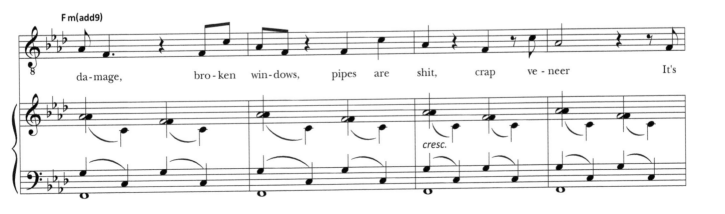

More intense

ho - urs la - ter Je - sus I'm still stand - ing here_____ Still

stand - ing_____ here_____ But when the

Slower 2 (♩=64)
Placid, calm and clear

sun - light hits the par - lor wall at cer - tain times of day I see how

fine this house could be_____ I see it so damn clear_____

Marcato (♩=♩), with ferocity

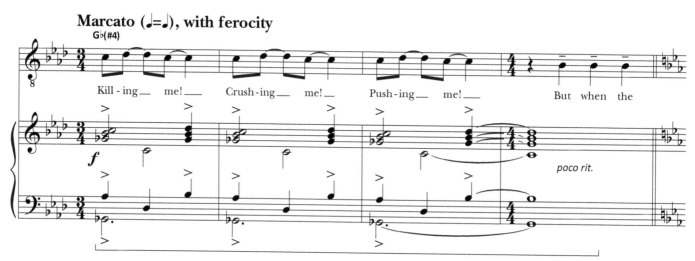

Slower 2 (♩=64)

Recit: Dark, alone

96

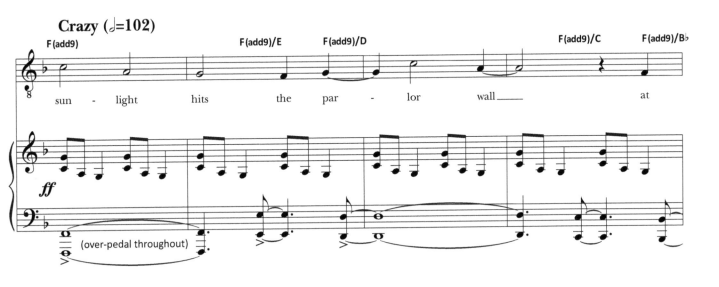

Flying Away
(Finale)

Music: Jeanine Tesori
Lyrics: Lisa Kron

Recit (Slow and considered)

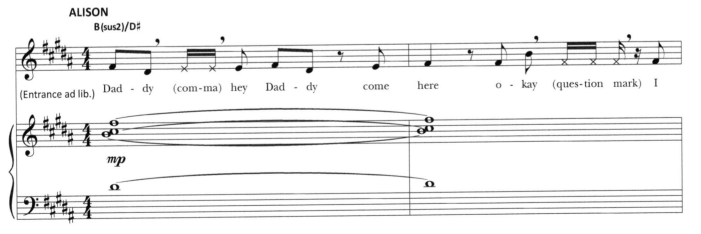

ALISON

(Entrance ad lib.) Dad - dy (com-ma) hey Dad - dy come here o - kay (ques-tion mark) I

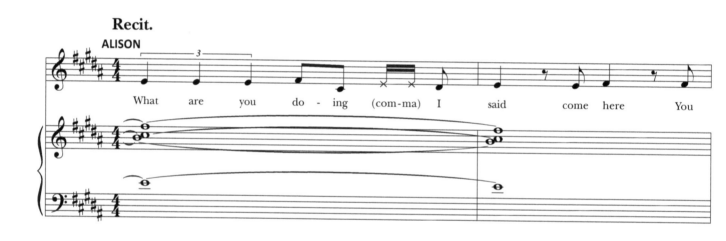

MEDIUM ALISON

SMALL ALISON

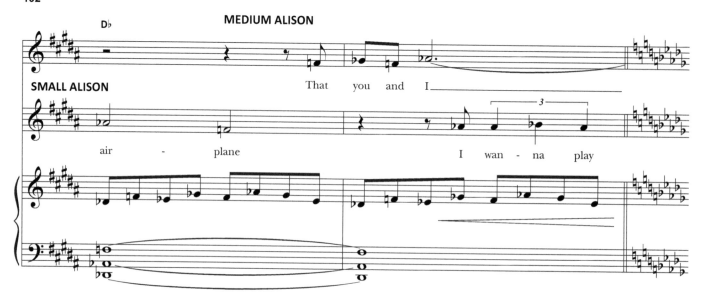

MEDIUM ALISON

SMALL ALISON. Like the Red Baron in his Sopwith Camel! No, wait--

was   like   you

SMALL ALISON

Like

MEDIUM ALISON

Ebm7

Say   some - thing!

SMALL ALISON

Su - per - man

ALISON

—up   in   the   sky   'Til   I   can   see

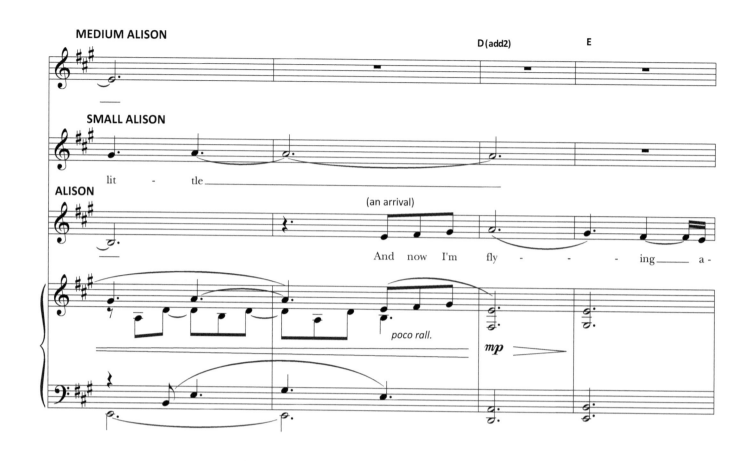

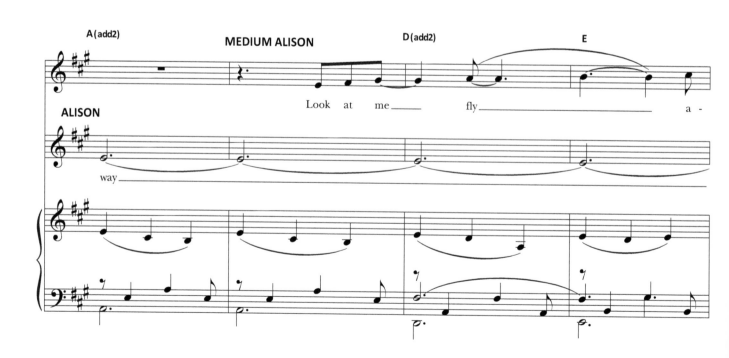

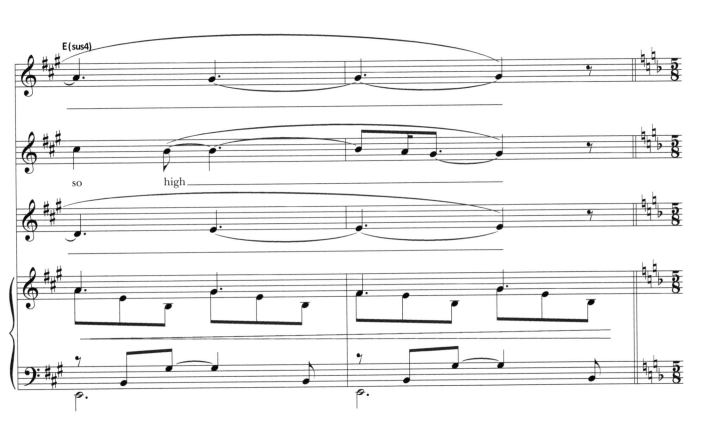

108

A Tempo, Full (a victory!)

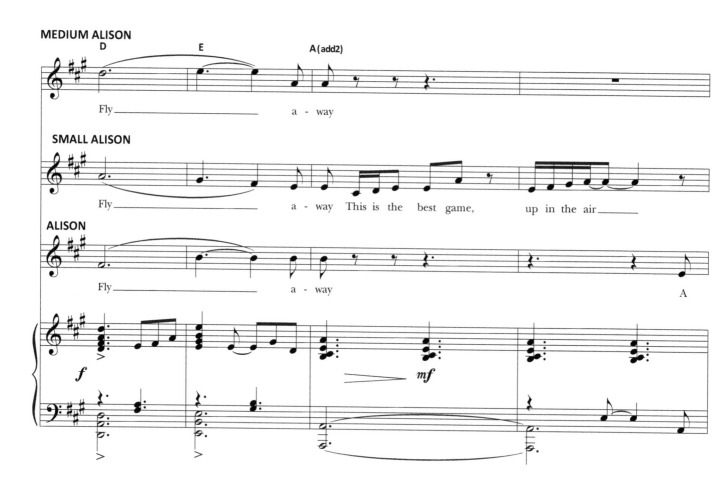

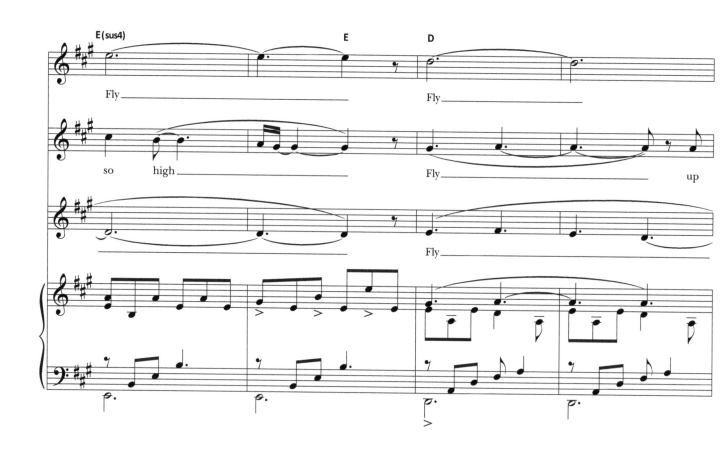

Pony Girl

Music: Jeanine Tesori
Lyrics: Lisa Kron

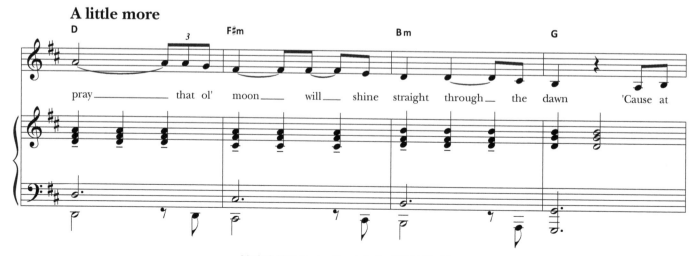

CREATIVE TEAM

JEANINE TESORI *(Music)* won the Tony Award for Best Original Score with Lisa Kron for the musical *Fun Home*, which is currently playing on Broadway. She has also written Tony-nominated scores for *Twelfth Night* at Lincoln Center; *Thoroughly Modern Millie* (lyrics, Dick Scanlan); *Caroline, or Change* (lyrics, Tony Kushner); and *Shrek The Musical* (lyrics, David Lindsay-Abaire). The production of *Caroline, or Change* at the National Theatre in London received the Olivier Award for Best New Musical. Her 1997 Off-Broadway musical *Violet* (lyrics, Brian Crawley) opened on Broadway in 2014 and garnered four Tony nominations, including Best Musical Revival. Opera: *A Blizzard on Marblehead Neck* (libretto, Tony Kushner; Glimmerglass) and *The Lion, The Unicorn, and Me* (libretto, J. D. McClatchy; Kennedy Center). Music for plays: *Mother Courage* (dir. George C. Wolfe, with Meryl Streep and Kevin Kline), John Guare's *A Free Man of Color* (Lincoln Center Theater, dir. George C. Wolfe), and *Romeo and Juliet* (Delacorte Gala). Film scores: *Nights in Rodanthe, Every Day*, and *You're Not You*. Ms. Tesori is a member of the Dramatists Guild and was cited by the ASCAP as the first female composer to have "two new musicals running concurrently on Broadway." She is the founding artistic director of Encores! Off-Center at New York City Center, and is a lecturer in music at Yale University and Columbia University. Most of all, she is the proud parent of Siena Rafter, a senior at LaGuardia High School for the Arts.

LISA KRON *(Book and Lyrics)* is a writer and performer whose work has been widely produced in New York, regionally, and internationally. She wrote the book and lyrics for musical *Fun Home*, with music by composer Jeanine Tesori, which won five 2015 Tony awards including Best Musical. It also received Lortel, Obie, Drama Critics Circle and Outer Critics Circle awards for best musical and was finalist for the Pulitzer Prize. Lisa's other plays include *The Ver**zon Play; In The Wake* (Lilly Award, Best Plays of 2010-2011); *Well* (Best Plays of 2003-2004, Lortel Best Play nom.); and *2.5 Minute Ride* (Obie, L.A. Drama-Logue and GLAAD Media Awards). Lisa is a Tony-nominated actor (*Well*) and received a Lortel Award as best featured actress for her performance as Mrs. Mi-Tzu and Mrs. Yang in the Foundry Theater's acclaimed production of *Good Person of Szechuan*. Other honors include Guggenheim, Sundance, and MacDowell fellowships, a Doris Duke Performing Artists Award, a Cal Arts/Alpert Award, a Helen Merrill Award, and grants from the Creative Capital Foundation and NYFA. Lisa's craft was honed in a formative decade spent as part of the now legendary WOW Café Theater. She is a proud founding member of the OBIE- and Bessie-Award-winning collaborative theater company The Five Lesbian Brothers whose plays include *The Secretaries, Oedipus at Palm Springs*, and *Brave Smiles*. She serves on the boards of the McDowell Colony, Sundance Institute, Lilly Awards, and on the Council of the Dramatists Guild of America.

Credits

Originally Produced on Broadway by

Fox Theatricals   Barbara Whitman

Carole Shorenstein Hays

Tom Casserly   Paula Marie Black   Latitude Link
Terry Schnuck/Jane Lane   The Forstalls

Nathan Vernon   Mint Theatricals   Elizabeth Armstrong
Jam Theatricals   Delman Whitney

and Kristin Caskey & Mike Isaacson

The world premiere production of FUN HOME was produced by
The Public Theater

Oskar Eustis, Artistic Director; Patrick Willingham, Executive Director

In New York City on October 22nd, 2013

FUN HOME was developed, in part, at the 2012 Sundance Institute Theatre Lab at White Oak and the
2012 Sundance Institute Theatre Lab at the Sundance Resort.

Milton Keynes UK
Ingram Content Group UK Ltd.
UKHW052055111023
430429UK00009B/74